FIREBEARS
The Rescue Team

Rhonda Gowler Greene

illustrated by Dan Andreasen

SCHOLASTIC INC.
New York Toronto London Auckland Sydney
Mexico City New Delhi Hong Kong Buenos Aires

ISBN-13: 978-0-545-05186-6
ISBN-10: 0-545-05186-X

12 11 10 9 8 7 6 5 4 3 2 1   8 9 10 11 12/0

Printed in the U.S.A.   40

First Scholastic printing, October 2007

Designed by Amy Manzo Toth

The artist used oil paint on gessoed illustration board to create the illustrations for this book.

In admiration, and memory, of firefighters everywhere
"humble heroes, bold and brave"
—R. G. G.

For little Katrina
—D. A.

Firebears
Work and wait
At Fire Station Number Eight.

Bears on call,
Night or day,
On the job without delay.

Kitchen sink,
  Plates and cups,
  Basket full of spotted pups.

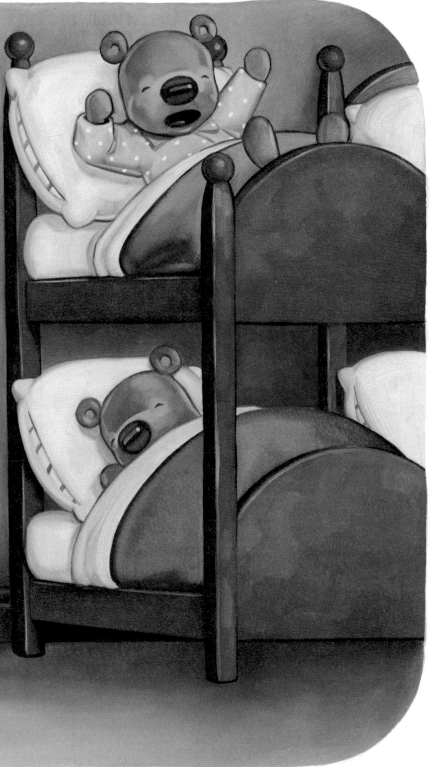

DING-LING-LING!
Through the hole.
Hurry, slip-slide down
the
pole!

Heavy coats,
Hats and boots,
Busy bears in fire suits.

Firebears
Speed through town,
Siren wailing up and down.

Racing, rushing
To the scene—
Firebears, the rescue team!

False alarm
At 103,
Scaredy-cat stuck up a tree.

Reach the top
Rung by rung,
Happy kisses, scratchy tongue.

Listen up.
Radio!
Urgent message—GO **GO GO!**

Firebears
Speed through town,
Siren wailing up and down.

Racing, rushing
To the scene—
Firebears, the rescue team!

Poplar Street . . .
Store ablaze!
Bears push through a smoky haze.

Grab the hose,
Silver spray,
Bears are coming. Clear the way!

Splutter, splash!
Fire's out.
"Hip-hooray!" the townsfolk shout.

Can't rest yet.
Radio!
Bears must hurry—GO GO GO!

Firebears
Speed through town,
Siren wailing up and down.

Racing, rushing
To the scene—
Firebears, the rescue team!

Round the bend
House on fire!
Raise the ladder—higher, higher!

Clouds of smoke
Billowing—
Firebears can't see a thing.

Someone yells,
"Over here!"
Help is coming. Never fear!

Busy bears,
Strong and fast.
Everyone's now safe at last.

Always ready
At the scene—
Firebears, the rescue team!

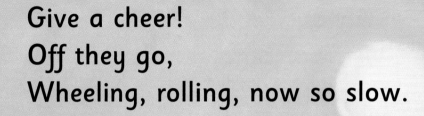

Give a cheer!
Off they go,
Wheeling, rolling, now so slow.

Weary bears
Smile and wave,
Humble heroes, bold and brave.

Back again
Through the gate . . .
At Fire Station Number Eight.